Dave Goes to Camp and Meets the Atlanteans

John D. Chichester

ISBN: 978-1-5356-1030-8

Introduction

Hello, my name is John D. Chichester. I'm a writer, and as everyone knows, writing has always been an important part of my life, and continues to be. Staying focused is the most important part of my life. Your most valuable quality is your foresight; that's what you set out to accomplish. It's an eye-of-the-tiger type of mentality. In order to achieve, you must first prepare your mind to conquer, because there will be many obstacles; that's a part of life we all have to deal with. Remember, though, in the face of adversity, stay vigilant and do not worry about others. It's all about you proving what you can do for yourself. Do you have what it takes? What is your true potential? That must be determined by you and you only. Arm your mind like a tank and your ammunition will be life's educational programs. Then you will be ready and set to blast through many of life's brick walls of obstacles to achieve your goals. But always remember, the most important part of a dream is making it into a reality. To succeed in New York City are the thoughts that I keep inside, but it's also the place where I live.

Dave Goes to Camp and Meets the Atlanteans

After the incident at the book club, the school semester was coming to an end and summertime was approaching. Dave, Freddy, Jake, and Macey were all anxiously looking forward to their summer vacation, with just a few more weeks of school time to go. On one particular day, during the seventh period of class, an announcement was made on the school intercom. It was Principal Green, who said, "To all students who want to sign up for our annual summer-camp trip to Bear Mountain: please report to the main office at three p.m."

Dave and his friends planned to sign up for the trip, so they all went to the main office. Conversations about what the trip would be like filled the air from students who were signing up to go.

"I'm so happy about this camp trip," said Macey.

"I've never been there, either," said Jake.

"I don't think any of us have ever been there," said Freddy. "So, I think we are all going to have a good time."

"OK, everyone," said Principal Green, "please hand in your parents' signature of approval sheets before signing your trip slips." It was a three-day outing, scheduled for the second week in June.

"Three whole days at Bear Mountain, this is going to be great!" said Jake.

"You bet," said Dave.

On the weekend before the trip the kids spent time with their families. The following Friday it was time to go to Bear Mountain.

"All right, students, line up and prepare to board the bus," said Principal Green.

Before the students boarded the bus, they said goodbye to their parents.

"Mom, I forgot my video game," said Dave.

"No, you didn't," said Mrs. Thomas. "I took it off the table when we were leaving." She also gave him a cell phone to call home when he needed to. "Have a good time, Dave," Mrs. Thomas said.

"Thanks, Mom, love you, see you when I get back!" Dave replied.

"Dave, Macey, Freddy, let's get in line," said Jake.

"Hi, Stacey," Macey said.

"What's up, guys?" Stacey said.

"Do you want to sit with us?" said Macey.

Stacey was a friend of Dave, Macey, Jake, and Freddy. They all lived in the same neighborhood. She was thirteen years old and was born in the United States. Stacey lived with her mother and father, who was Native American Indians. They were professional chefs. Stacey also had an older brother and sister who worked and went to school. She loved her family and enjoyed spending time with them when they were not so busy working or going to school.

Dave Thomas was fourteen years old. He was born in the United States. He lived with his parents, Mr. and Mrs. Thomas, who were also born in the United States. His mother was African American. She was a train conductor for the New York State Transit Authority. Mr. Thomas was African American and a New Jersey State Police officer. Playing basketball, being with family, and hanging out with his best friends were some of Dave's favorite things to do.

Macey Davis was fourteen years old. She was an American citizen. Her family was from Italy. Macey had an inquisitive personality and liked to write poetry and short stories. She lived with her older sister and her mother, who was a licensed dentist with her own dental office. Macey loved her mother very much because she worked hard to provide for her family.

Jake Lee was thirteen years old. He lived in New Jersey with his mother and father, who were Asian Americans. Mr. and Mrs. Lee worked for a video-game-software company, editing new games before they were sold in stores. This explained why Jake loved video games. He knew all the latest games out.

Freddy Santos was a thirteen-year-old born in America who lived in New Jersey with his parents, Maria and Jose Santos, who came from Puerto Rico. They were owners of a sneaker store, selling the latest in footwear. Freddy liked to ride his bicycle and play basketball with his older brother. He was also a very kind person and tended to have a little sense of humor, like his friends.

"All right, everyone," said Principal Green, "sit down and buckle up your seat belts." The bus was filled with the sounds of laughter and kids talking with each other, some of them listening to music on their headphones and playing video games. Meanwhile, the bus was already on its way.

"How long will it take us to get there?" Freddy asked Principal Green.

"Why do you have to ask her that? Just sit back and enjoy the ride," Macey said.

"It's all right, Macey," said Principal Green. "We'll be there in an hour or two, Freddy. You guys will have fun, there are lots of things to do and lots of food at the campsite."

"How do you like that, Principal Green is talking about eating and I'm feeling a little hungry myself," said Macey.

Time went by as the bus came closer to its destination. The atmosphere on the bus was very calm. Some of the kids were calm, and some of them were looking out the windows, enjoying the scenery. Principal Green was sitting in front, talking with one of the teachers. After a few more miles the bus finally reached the park.

"We're here, we're here," said Stacey.

"Wow, look at the mountains," said Dave.

"And the huge trees," said Freddy.

"Stay in your seats until the bus stops," Principal Green said.

"Bear Mountain, we're finally here," said Dave.

"Good," said Jake, "cause I have to use the bathroom."

When the students got off the bus they were greeted by the camp counselors and staff.

"Hello everyone, welcome to Bear Mountain Camp Resort. I'm the head counselor, Mrs. Davenport. This is Mrs. Black, Mrs. Jefferies, Mrs. Tomkins, and Mr. Berns. Here at Bear Mountain we have two huge cabins. Cabin One is where we have the cafeteria for you to eat, and a recreation area with arcade games for you to play and other fun activities," Mrs. Davenport said. "Cabin Two is for sleeping and showering."

"When can we eat, Mrs. Davenport?" said Macey.

"You can put your belongings in your rooms and then come over to the cafeteria for lunch," Mrs. Jefferies said.

"Let's hurry up, guys," Macey said. "I'll go to my room and we'll meet in the cafeteria."

"Yeah, I wanna go to the arcade after lunch," said Jake.

"I'll be there too," said Dave.

"Don't forget about me," said Freddy, "I love playing video games too."

"This is cool, all three of us in the same room," said Dave. "Wow, our windows have a great view. You can see the mountains, trees, and birds flying everywhere."

"That's cool, Dave," said Freddy, "but we have to go to lunch to meet Macey and then go check out the arcade games."

So, to Cabin One all the students went. As they entered the lunchroom the guys saw Macey and Stacey sitting at the first table.

"All this great food. Hey look, my favorite, hamburgers," said Jake.

"And fried chicken," said Freddy.

"I like hamburgers and fried chicken too, guys. But fruits and vegetables are very healthy for you. That's what my mom says," said Dave.

After putting their food on their trays the boys walked over to sit with Macey and Stacey.

"Finally, you guys made it," said Macey.

"Sorry about that, Macey," said Dave. "There was so much food, it took us a little time deciding what we wanted."

While the students ate their lunch, there was an announcement made by Principal Green, who entered the room with the head counselor, Mrs. Davenport, and the recreation counselor, Mr. Berns. It was the schedule for tomorrow's sightseeing and games events. The time for eating was over and the fun at the arcade began. Leaving some students behind still eating, Dave and his friends walked into another large room.

"Wow, the arcade room," said Jake.

"They have about eight games here," said Freddy.

"They also have two pinball games," said Macey.

"Let's play the pinball machine, Macey," said Stacey. "We'll be over there."

Dave, Jake, and Freddy were finally playing the arcade games. Other students were watching movies and participating in other activities as the warm spring day gave way to a cool spring night, giving the kids a bird's eye view of the night sky.

It was around seven p.m. when the kids were instructed by camp staff to go to their cabin for the rest of the night. They were to take their showers and get plenty of rest. They also ate dinner before they went to their rooms.

"Look at all the stars in the sky," said Dave as he walked with his friends back to their cabin.

"We can't even see all the stars like this back in Jersey," said Freddy.

"Hey look, a shooting star," said Jake.

"That's amazing," said Stacey. "It's really a small meteorite burning up as it enters the earth's atmosphere."

"How did you know that?" asked Jake.

"I like to watch the science channel," Stacey said.

"That's really cool," said Dave, "but it's time for all of us to get some rest. We have a big day tomorrow."

"Yeah, this is definitely going to be fun," said Macey.

Principal Green and Mrs. Davenport were standing in the hall by a small office near the entrance, informing everyone entering the cabin that there were telephones available in the office if they needed to call home.

"Two counselors, Mr. Berns and Mrs. Tompkins, will be here throughout the night," said the head counselor. "Get lots of rest. We have a busy day ahead of us."

Sounds of happy talk filled the cabin hall. Then silence entered as the students retreated to their rooms. "See you guys in the morning," said Stacey and Macey.

"OK," "Later," "See you tomorrow," said the guys.

The hours went by. Everyone was asleep except for the camp counselors, who were on their rounds checking each room, making sure the kids were sleeping.

Night came to an end, replaced by the shining sun revealing a bright spring morning. The air was filled with birds. It was a day for fun and at seven a.m. the camp counselors were busy moving from room to room, waking all the students.

"Good morning, Mrs. Black," said Dave, Jake, and Freddy.

"Well, you guys are some early birds," Mrs. Black said.

"We're just excited about the fun time we're going to have today," said Dave.

"Yes, Dave," Mrs. Black said, "we do have some fun-filled activities scheduled for everyone today. But before all of that you kids have to eat a healthy breakfast."

When they finished brushing their teeth, taking their showers, and getting dressed, Dave, Jake, and Freddy were ready to go to the cafeteria. Then there was a *knock knock* on the door.

"Come in," said Jake. It was Stacey and Macey. "What's up, guys?"

"Morning, guys," said Macey and Stacey.

"We're ready to go," said Stacey.

"Let's get out of here," said Jake.

They walked over to the cafeteria. The students were proceeding to enter when they were greeted by Principal Green and the camp staff.

"Good morning, everyone," said Mrs. Davenport.

"Hi guys, how are you all doing this morning?" Mr. Berns said.

"Good morning, Mrs. Davenport," said Stacey.

"Morning, Mr. Berns," said Dave. "Are we going to do some hiking today?"

"Yes, Dave, we're going to have a lot of fun, but you kids should eat a healthy, balanced breakfast to get your energy up before we do any activities," Mr. Berns said.

Eventually everyone was eating breakfast while Principal Green called names from a list to make sure all students were present. The cafeteria was getting noisy so Head Counselor Davenport raised her voice and said, "Quiet down, everyone, quiet down, Counselor Berns has something to say."

"OK," said Mr. Berns, "listen up. When you're all finished eating, report outside. We'll be getting ready for today's activities."

"Hey, Jake," said Macey, "take your time and eat, the food isn't going anywhere."

"Ha ha ha," laughed Freddy, Stacey, and Dave.

"Guys, before we go outside," said Dave, "there's something I would like to tell you."

"What is it?" said Macey.

"Yeah, what happened, Dave?" said Freddy.

"Tell us," said Jake.

"All right," Dave said. "Last night before I went to sleep, I decided to look out the window to check out the scenery. Suddenly, in the darkness behind the trees, I saw a bright light shining through. Then I saw two objects rising above the trees. The objects continue to rise higher into the air."

Dave explained that the two crafts were round with three different-colored lights blinking in a circular motion.

"Wow," said Stacey. "What else did you see, Dave?"

"Not much after that," Dave said. "They just stood still in the air and did not make a sound. Even when they zoomed off into the black skies with great speed, there was no sound. Promise me, guys, that you won't tell anyone about this," said Dave. "Not Principal Green or any of the camp counselors."

"Who would believe us anyway?" said Jake.

"That's some story, Dave," said Macey.

"Yeah," said Freddy, "I believe you saw something but you should've woken me and Jake to see also."

"That's it, I know what you saw!" said Stacey. "It was a UFO."

"What's a UFO?" asked Jake.

"It's an unidentified flying object," Macey said.

"You mean like a flying saucer?" said Freddy.

"Correct," said Stacey.

"Your story is definitely out of this world, Dave," Freddy said.

"Listen up, guys, we need to stop talking about this for now and concentrate on having some fun on this nice warm and sunny Saturday morning," Dave said.

"Dave is right," said Macey, "we came on this trip to have fun and I'm not going to let this flying saucer stuff stop us from enjoying the weekend. Come on, let's join the other students outside."

Finally, everyone was together, and Mrs. Davenport and all the counselors were waiting.

"OK, everybody," said Mrs. Davenport, "I need you all to form two lines."

While the students formed two lines they noticed the different games that were set up for them to play.

"I wonder what we will do first," said Dave.

"I think we'll go hiking first," said Macey.

"How do you know?" asked Jake.

"She's right," said Stacey, "I asked one of the counselors earlier and she said hiking is first."

Principal Green made an announcement giving instructions about what to do and what not to do. Then at last everyone was on their way. The kids enjoyed a day of hiking and sightseeing from high mountain areas. Also, the view of the Hudson River from upstate New York to New York City was amazing.

"This is great," said Dave. "I can't believe this view."

"Yeah," said Jake, "I can't believe we are so high up."

"I never thought I would be able to look at the Hudson River from a position on a mountain that's also a national park," Macey said.

"Yes," said Stacey, "the river looks small from here. I can see how it's shaped."

"Well," said Jake, "we've seen a lot except a bear, which would go perfectly with the name of this park, Bear Mountain."

"Very funny," said Freddy. "I bet you would jump out of your pants if you were to see a bear."

"All right, everybody," said Counselor Tompkins, "we will be heading back to the cabin for you kids to eat your lunch. Now I need you all to form two lines. After eating lunch, go to the activities ground, and for the rest of the afternoon you all can play. The arcade room is also available if anyone wants to come inside."

The day went very well for all the students. Some stayed outside to play games like volleyball and basketball. Some played catch with the softball, and some went to the arcade to play video games, like Jake and Freddy, who decided to leave Dave, Macey, and Stacey outside.

"I'm done," said Jake.

"Yeah, me too," said Freddy. "Playing basketball really makes me thirsty."

"You're not the only one who's thirsty," said Jake. "Let's go to the cafeteria to get something to drink."

"Hey, what's up?" said Dave. "Where are you guys going?"

"We're going to get something to drink and then we're going to play some video games in the arcade," Freddy said.

"Cool," said Dave. "I'll play some more volleyball with Stacey and Macey. Then we'll come hang out with you guys."

"OK," said Jake, "see you in a little while."

The students continued to play outside and have fun in the arcade room for the rest of the day. At five o'clock in the evening they all went to dinner and enjoyed a meal of their choice.

"Wow," said Stacey, "that was a great dinner."

"I know," said Macey, "with all the moving around we were doing we definitely worked up an appetite."

"Hey, Dave," said Jake, "you still thinking about what you saw last night?"

"Yes, Dave," Freddy said, "that was an amazing story you told us."

"It's not a story," said Dave, "I really saw it."

"Well, I don't know about you guys," said Stacey, "but I believe him."

"I believe you too," Macey said, "but I would like to see it for myself."

"Maybe we can," said Freddy.

"What are you talking about?" asked Dave.

"Guys, I have a plan," Freddy said.

"What plan?" asked Macey.

"Tonight, when everyone is asleep, we will not go to sleep. Instead we will stay up and look through the window," said Freddy. "Macey and Stacey, you two can contact me, Jake, and Dave on your cell phone."

"That's a good idea," said Dave, "but I would like to see these things a bit closer this time than just from the window."

"But that means we would have to go outside to see them closer," Jake said.

"And how are we going to do that with the camp counselors there?" asked Macey.

"I know how," said Stacey. "I've noticed the counselors take a break when everyone gets settled in their rooms."

"We'll have to keep checking for when they leave," said Dave.

Meanwhile, in the cafeteria, the students finished their dinner.

"Attention, students," said Principal Green with Mrs. Davenport by her side. "We hope you had a great day and a wonderful dinner. In a few minutes, everyone will have to go to their rooms for a good night's rest."

"You all have a busy day tomorrow," Mrs. Davenport said.

As the students began to leave the cafeteria the darkness of night began to descend upon the warm spring evening. For Dave, Macey, Jake, Freddy, and their friend Stacey, there was something on their minds other than going to sleep.

"Hello, everyone," said Mrs. Jefferies, with Mrs. Tompkins standing by her side.

"Hi, Mrs. Jefferies, hi, Mrs. Tompkins," was said by most of the students as they entered the door on their way to their rooms.

Dave and his friends were the last to enter the cabin. They did this purposely because they wanted to ask the camp counselors one question.

"Hi, Mrs. Jefferies," said Macey.

"Hi, Macey," said Mrs. Jefferies and Mrs. Tompkins.

"Goodnight, Mrs. Jefferies," said Stacey.

"Mrs. Jefferies, can I ask you a question?" asked Macey.

"Yes, Macey what is it?" asked Mrs. Jefferies.

"Do you guys take a break on your job during the night? Like someone who takes a break on their job during the day?"

"Yes, Macey," Mrs. Jefferies said, "we take two breaks, one at ten o'clock and the other at twelve, for thirty minutes."

This was exactly what the kids wanted to hear. They bid Mrs. Jefferies goodnight and went to their rooms, satisfied with the answers they'd received. The kids now knew the time they would leave the dorm.

"Now we know what time they're leaving," said Dave.

"Yeah, and what time we will be leaving," said Jake.

"Hey, Dave," said Freddy, "your phone is ringing. It's got to be Macey or Stacey."

"Hello?" said Dave.

"Hey, Dave," said Macey.

"What's up, Macey?" said Dave.

"Make sure you guys are ready at ten o'clock," Macey said.

"Don't worry, we will be ready," Dave said.

The time for action was at hand. Getting into trouble with the school principal and camp counselors was a risk the five friends were willing to take.

At ten o'clock the counselors took their break. The coast was clear. The five friends left their rooms and out of the cabin they went, silently and quickly.

"OK, guys," said Macey, "now that we're outside—"

"I know," said Jake, "let me ask that question. What direction are we going in, Dave? Going into a forest at night is not my idea of a good time," said Jake.

"I agree with you," said Dave, "but that's where I saw the object with the lights."

"Let's go, guys, before someone spots us," said Macey. "I hope that someone isn't Principal Green," Freddy said.

"We're here…" said Stacey.

"Dave, what do we do now?" asked Jake.

"We wait to see if they will come again," Dave said.

"This place is beginning to give me the creeps," said Freddy.

"Yeah," said Stacey, "all those sounds coming from the forest."

"Those are the sounds of nocturnal animals," said Dave.

"What are nocturnal animals?" asked Freddy. "Hey, I remember, they are creatures that love the night and come out to hunt for food at night. Like bats, owls, wolves, spiders, and many more."

"That's good to know," said Jake, "so we will stay out of their way and they won't come hunting for us."

Meanwhile, back at the cabin, the counselors returned from their break, not knowing the students were outside in the woods.

"What time is it?" asked Freddy.

"It's ten thirty," said Macey.

"We've been here for half an hour," said Jake, "and the longer we stay the creepier this place gets."

"Hey, what's that over there?" said Macey. Suddenly the dark forest was exposed to a bright shining light that seemed to be moving in the children's direction.

"The light is getting closer to us, we have to leave," said Jake.

"No," said Macey, "we've come too far and risked getting into trouble already. It will all be for nothing!"

As the light moved closer to the kids they could clearly see where it was coming from.

"Hey, look at that," said Macey.

"It looks like a spacecraft," said Dave, "and that's what I saw through the window. Look at the different-colored lights around it shining so bright."

"Yeah," said Stacey, "there's

red, blue, and yellow, and they're all blinking at different times."

As the object got closer, the kids could finally see it clearly.

"A huge triangle," said Macey. "What a shape for a spacecraft."

"The light is getting closer to being right over us," Freddy said.

"It's over our heads right now," said Jake.

"Let's get out of here," said Dave.

But before they could move they found themselves unable to move. The spacecraft hovered directly over them with a powerful beam of white light stopping them in their tracks.

"What is this?" asked Stacey.

"We're being lifted off the ground," said Jake.

"Yes, but by who or by what?" asked Dave.

"I think we're about to find that out up close and personal," said Freddy.

Within an instant, the kids were pulled up into the strange craft, leaving no trace of them ever being in the forest. The bright white light retracted back into the craft.

"Where are we?" said Macey.

"I think we're in the spaceship," said Stacey.

"That light pulled us into this ship," said Jake.

"What kind of room is this? Look at all the strange markings on the walls," said Freddy.

"Egyptian hieroglyphics, that's what it seems like to me," Dave said. "This room is the color of silver with gold linings and markings."

"Only one entrance," said Macey, "in or out."

The kids began to wonder who was flying the craft they were now trapped in and where they were.

"We need to get out of this room," said Dave.

"This door does not open like a regular door," said Macey.

"This door slides in and out like in *Star Trek*," Stacey said.

Suddenly the door opened automatically, shocking everyone. They all looked at each other, not saying a word, waiting to see who would take the first step out of the room.

Suddenly they heard a voice that said, "Come on out, my friends, don't be afraid."

"Who is that speaking to us?" asked Jake.

"I think they can see us," said Dave.

"We can also hear you," said the voice.

"Where do you want us to go?" asked Dave.

"When you leave the room," said the voice, "and go into the hall of the ship, make a right and keep walking. Continue walking until you see two doors. Turn toward your right and enter. It will open," said the voice.

"I hope we can remember all of that," said Freddy.

"Don't worry," said Stacey, "I remember."

"I wonder how they will look," said Macey.

"Probably like space aliens," said Jake.

As the five friends walked through the hall toward the room, they couldn't help noticing the many Egyptian-type hieroglyphics on the walls, which, as Dave had pointed out, were metallic silver with gold linings.

"I think whoever is flying this ship is very tall," Macey said.

"How do you know that?" asked Freddy.

"Haven't you guys noticed, this is a large spacecraft," said Dave.

When the kids reached the room, they'd been told to go to, great anticipation filled their minds. They wondered who these creatures were and what they looked like.

"Here we go," said Stacey.

"Wow," Jake said, "look at the size of this room."

"Silver-colored with gold linings, like the other room we were in," said Freddy.

"This must be the main part of the ship," said Dave.

"You mean like the room the pilot and copilot sit in to fly an airplane?" Jake said.

Suddenly the voice appeared again. This time it was coming from someone in the room.

"Hello, my friends, welcome," said the voice.

"Where is he?" asked Macey.

"Who is that?" said Jake. "And look at how tall he is."

"He looks like a giant man," Freddy said.

"Check out his skin color," said Stacey. "It's like dark red."

"Look at all the gold they're wearing," said Macey. "And he's dressed like the ancient Egyptians."

As the kids moved closer to get a better look at this person, who looked totally out of this world to them, they noticed that there were others like him. But unlike him, they were sitting, moving their hands, pressing digital images on small screens in front of them that in turn connected the data to a huge screen. "Check out those guys over there," said Stacey.

"I think they are flying the ship," said Dave.

"That makes sense," said Macey. "We are in the main part of the ship."

"Who are you? And where did you come from?" Dave asked.

"My name is Asapha, and my people and I are from the Earth, just like you. But not from the Earth you know. We are from a time when the

Earth and its population looked totally different from the Earth of your time. We are Atlanteans from the great lands of Atlantis," Asapha said, "from the ancient past."

"But how did you get here from the past?" asked Macey.

"It's a long story, one which we don't have enough time with you to tell," Asapha said.

"OK," said Jake, "but tell us how you got here from the past."

"We are time travelers moving through the space-time continuum," Asapha said. "Our great land was destroyed by the mighty death ray, which caused volcanic fires, earthquakes, and floods. The technology from our home before its destruction is what we use to travel and carry our culture and science with us everywhere we go."

"Yes, I understand," said Dave. "You are talking about this great time-traveling spaceship. It was built in Atlantis, wasn't it?"

"Yes, my friend, it was," said Asapha, "before the fall."

"You can call me Dave. These are my best friends, Jake, Macey, Freddy, and Stacey."

"So, you guys have everything you need here," said Macey, "but how do you keep the power going?"

"Our ship runs on the negative and positive forces of nature," Asapha said. "That's pure energy tapped from the sun itself and transferred to the Quartz Stone, which stores vast amounts of cosmic energy. Enough for us to travel for many years before repowering. This craft was also built anti to gravity," Asapha said.

"What does that mean?" asked Jake.

"To put it simply, gravity is like a magnet pulling anything that's physical toward it. This ship creates the same level of magnetic force as gravity, making it totally resistant to the pulling force of gravity," Asapha said. "Remember that the same sides of two magnets have the same pulling force but can never touch, only repel. We also gather materials from the many places we travel to, whether it's the past, present, future, or the many planets throughout space that we visit."

There was something else that caught the attention of the children. On the wall of the room there were perfectly carved pyramids.

"These pyramid carvings represent a time in human history before the Egyptians, Greeks, Romans, Mayans, Aztecs, and all others," Asapha said, "the second and third waves of humanity, who were like giants in size compared to the human beings in your present time. They also possessed a third eye. They were the Lemurians, from the land of Mu, also called Easter Island in your present time. The Atlanteans in particular were highly advanced human beings," Asapha said. "Their technology was highly superior to the technology of your time, young Macey."

"What do you mean by superior?" asked Freddy.

"He means it was better," said Dave.

"Think about it, guys, he doesn't need to explain everything," Stacey said. "This huge spaceship tells it all."

"Yes, she's right," said Jake. "I mean, there's no one in our present time who can travel back and forth through time and space."

"Asapha," said Dave, "I noticed you are the only one speaking; the others are not speaking."

"They can speak," Asapha said, "but we don't have to speak if we don't want to. Because we Atlanteans can talk with our minds to each other."

"What kinds of buildings did you guys have in Atlantis?" asked Dave. "Were they huge?"

"Yes," said Asapha. "We built many pyramids and round circular structures. The age of pyramid building began in Atlantis. The Atlanteans were master architects and master builders and, once again, they built big structures. All sank into the ocean when Atlantis was destroyed. But most of these buildings were sealed shut by the masters. Waiting for the right time to be discovered by human beings of your time and in the distant future. These discoveries will raise humanity to a brighter, more technologically advanced age when they discover what's inside of them," Asapha said. "Atlantis did not sink all at once, though it took some years. Many escaped, carrying their higher science and knowledge of building pyramids across different parts of the Earth. They also flew in their airships. These ships can travel underwater and throughout space."

"Can you tell us what other parts of the Earth your people went to live on?" asked Dave.

"Well, Dave," Asapha said, "the lands presently called India, Mexico, Peru, and Chile. Also, the great lands of the Americas and the great lands of the Orients."

"What about people like the Aztecs, the Mayans, and Incas?" said Macey. "We learned about them in school. In our time, it's a great mystery as to how their mighty pyramids and great structures were built. It was the Atlanteans, wasn't it?"

"Yes, Macey," Asapha said. "We were the only ones who had the technology and higher science to do this."

"What about Stonehenge in Europe?" asked Jake."Yes, that structure was built by the Atlanteans, who lived in many parts of Europe before it was even called Europe," Asapha said. "The continent of Africa was heavily populated by the Atlanteans. The people of that land were also influenced by Atlantean culture and higher-science knowledge."

"Hey," said Freddy, "I know! Egypt, right?"

"Of course," said Dave, "the Great Pyramid of Giza and the Sphinx." "Yes, my friends," Asapha said, "those two mighty structures were built by an Atlantean Sage and by the mysterious demigod Hermes, who was the architect, with the help of the Nubian people, who were the original citizens of that land when the Atlanteans arrived."

"What is it like traveling back and forth through time?" asked Jake.

"Well, as a matter of fact, Jake," Asapha said, "we are traveling through time right now."

When the children heard that they were traveling through time into the distant past, to Egypt to see the Great Pyramid of Giza when it was first built, they were very excited but couldn't help wondering how they could not feel the effects of time traveling.

"Asapha," Macey said, "how come we are not affected by this time traveling stuff?"

"Our ship was built from rare unknown metals to withstand any environment we travel through. This includes deep space, the ocean, and, of course, time traveling," Asapha said. "These metals are on Earth but have not been discovered by the people of your time yet."

"Hey, guys," said Dave, "I think we are here."

The huge screen on the ship was like a window. Everyone could see the outside, and it was Egypt, thousands of years in the past. As the ship moved in for a closer view, over the horizon they could see the peak of the Great Pyramid.

"There it is," said Macey.

"Yeah," said Stacey, "I can see it too."

"It must be really big if we can see it from this far," said Freddy.

"The ship is getting closer," said Jake. "Too bad we can't go outside.""I think we can't go outside," said Dave, "because it can mess up history and change our futures. Also, we might be seen by the people of this time."

The ship finally reached the Great Pyramid, hovering high in the air. To the ancient people below it would look like a small object unmoving in the day sky."Wow, look at the size of it," said Stacey.

"It's so shiny," said Macey, "looking like a glass pyramid."

"Or a giant light bulb," said Freddy, "from the sun's reflection."

"Yeah, Asapha," Jake asked, "why is it so shiny?"

"Well, Jake," Asapha said, "limestone, which is strong and long-lasting, was part of the Great Pyramid's make-up, perfectly cut and smoothed out with laser tools, giving the structure its glassy, shiny look."

"How long did it take to get built?" asked Dave.

"It took one hundred years to build this amazing structure," Asapha said.

"What did they use to put these giant stones together like perfectly fitted Lego blocks?" asked Macey.

"Specially tuned handheld devices were used to levitate the stones and put them into place. They were fused together with laser tools. They also used airships to lift the stones and place them at the top."

"Thank you for showing us a piece of history in the making, Asapha," said Dave.

"Yes," said Macey, "thank you, but I think we should be going back to our time at the campsite."

"But we've been gone for a long time," said Stacey. "We're going to be in trouble."

"She's right," said Jake, "how are we going to get back to camp without anyone seeing us?"

"Do not worry, everyone," Asapha said, "we will take you back in time to the point where we picked you up."

"That's great," said Freddy. "The camp counselors went on break before we left. We'll be able to sneak into the cabin when they take their break.

As they prepared to time travel back to the future, on the ship's viewing screen the group saw a crowd of people gathering on the ground around the Great Pyramid. Asapha ordered his crew to view in a bit closer to see what they were doing. To their surprise, the people in the crowd were raising their hands, pointing up toward the ship.

"They can see us, I mean the ship," said Dave.

"We should be leaving now," said Macey.

"Yes," said Asapha.

The craft began to move forward from the Great Pyramid. Suddenly it shot off with great speed, disappearing from the sight of the onlookers. Within minutes they'd returned from the past to the present."Hey guys, look," said Stacey, "we're back at Bear Mountain."

"All right," said Jake, "it's nighttime, we've returned before the counselors come back from their break."

As the kids bid Asapha and his companions farewell, he made a promise that he would return to see them again since they were now his trusted friends. He also told them to return to the room they'd first entered on the ship. So, they did, and they were instantly teleported into the forest behind the campsite. The kids hurried into the cabin.

They spent the rest of their time at Bear Mountain having fun, promising amongst themselves not to tell anyone about the most amazing adventure they had ever experienced. But no one would ever believe them. They also realized that they had a lot to tell their families.

www.ingramcontent.com/pod-product-compliance
Lightning Source LLC
LaVergne TN
LVHW010550100826
845148LV00013B/2682

* 9 7 8 1 5 3 5 6 1 0 3 0 8 *